This our Planet

Written by Rob Alcraft

Collins

Our planet is full of life.
You can find life in all kinds of environments.

desert environment

hot

Arctic environment

freezing

3

Sunshine and heat

Big parts of our planet are desert. Life is difficult in this hot and hostile environment.

camel riders

Deserts can be roasting hot in the day, and freezing at night!

Wild forest

Wild forests are important environments for our planet.

Wildlife can hide and feed in the trees.

squirrel

little owl

High peaks

Lines of peaks reach up high.
On steep hillsides, you might spot kites
hunting their prey.

Ibexes are wild goats that can survive high up.

Wide plains

Animals can travel for miles across the wide plains.

Lions hunt and herds of zebras graze here.

The name for a pack of lions is a pride.

Arctic chill

In the Arctic, it might seem bleak and hostile. But you can still find animals that survive here.

Arctic fox

sea otter

seal

13

Fields

Just a tenth of our planet is farmland.

But so much food comes from fertile fields like this.

combine harvester

Coast and beach

There can be lots of houses on the hillsides and along the coastline.

People like to travel and fish from boats on the sea.

Town

Towns are important for people's lives.
People drive in, or ride on buses and trains.

Towns are ideal for shopping, playing and jobs of all kinds.

tram

We have just the one planet

We must keep our planet and all its environments safe.

The environments on our planet

After reading

Letters and Sounds: Phase 5

Word count: 249

Focus phonemes: /ai/ ay, ey, a-e /ee/ ie, ea /igh/ i, i-e

Common exception words: of, you, all, to, the, full, are, be, one, have, so, houses, our, their, people, here, comes, there, we, little

Curriculum links: Human and physical geography

National Curriculum learning objectives: Reading/word reading: read other words of more than one syllable that contain taught GPCs; Reading/comprehension: understand both the books they can already read accurately and fluently and those they listen to by checking that the text makes sense to them as they read, and correcting inaccurate reading

Developing fluency

- Your child may enjoy hearing you read the book.
- Take turns to read a page. Read with enthusiasm and excitement to encourage your child to read with expression too. Check they read the labels.

Phonic practice

- Focus on the /ee/ and /igh/ sounds.
- Look together at pages 12 and 13. Challenge your child to find two words in which the /ee/ sound is written differently. (*seem; bleak, sea, seal*) Turn to page 15. Can your child find the /ee/ sound written differently? (*fields*)
- Ask your child to read these words, and then identify the letter or letters that make the /igh/ sound.

  ibexes   hillsides   coastline   kinds

Extending vocabulary

- Can your child think of an antonym (opposite) for the following?

  bleak (e.g. *cheerful, colourful*)

  hostile (e.g. *friendly, welcoming*)

  fertile (e.g. *infertile, barren*)